LOVECATION
31 Days, 62 Positions

written by
Kiti Raynes

*To all of the Lovers who are seeking old and new ways
to explore each other while expressing affection
to keep the home fires burning
so their flames never get too low.*

LOVECATION:
31 DAYS, 62 POSITIONS

Written By
Kiti Raynes

Proofread By
Ukirah Yasmine

Fullcover Design By
Sun Child Wind Spirit

Edited By
Mylia Tiye Mal Jaza

LOVECATION: 31 Days, 62 Positions

Softcover ISBN-10: 3041996790   Softcover ISBN-13: 9780583547154

Hardcover ISBN-10: 6012724217   Hardcover ISBN-13: 9780291420923

Author Contact
Kiti Raynes
Copiah County, MSi
c/o The Writers Consortium
writersconsortium@bepublished.biz

Self-Publishing Associate
BePublished.Org - Chicago
(972) 880-8316
Dr. Mary Jefferson
P.O. Box 8324
Jackson, MS 39284
www.bepublished.org
publisher@bepublished.org

First Edition.
Printed In the USA.
Recycled Paper Encouraged.

THE WRITERS CONSORTIUM
www.WritersConsortium.us

TABLE OF CONTENT

Invitation

Sacred, Pleasure, Science

There are getaways... and then there are Lovecations. A Lovecation is more than a vacation around your love expressions. It's a sensual vow, a romantic pact to explore each other's bodies, desires, and fantasies for 31 days straight. This book is your guide. Your map. Your invitation. Whether you're reigniting a long-standing flame or basking in new lust with your soulmate, the Lovecation offers "Daily Duets" (two positions a day) intentionally chosen to draw you closer in every way.

Love is not meant to survive in silence. It craves rhythm. It begs for touch. It flourishes in skin-to-skin communion where trust meets trembling, and laughter dances between moans. Prepare to awaken, tease, ravish, and melt into each other.

LOVECATION is not just a book of sex positions (which I call "Love Postures"). It's a ritual. A commitment. A journey through the art and science of erotic connection between committed partners.

In a world that often pulls us in every direction — work, children, technology, stress — many couples find themselves distant not because they've fallen out of love, but because they've fallen out of sync. Regular, intentional, pleasure-focused intimacy isn't just pleasurable — it's essential.

What the Experts Say

1. Sex Strengthens the Bond

According to Dr. Justin Lehmiller, a social psychologist and researcher at the Kinsey Institute:

"Couples who maintain a healthy sex life often report higher satisfaction with their relationship overall, and tend to be more resilient during times of conflict or stress."

His research shows that sexual frequency and satisfaction are directly linked to emotional closeness and conflict resolution in long-term couples [Lehmiller, 2021].

2. Sexual Intimacy Boosts Health

A study published in the Journal of Health and Social Behavior found that older adults who maintained regular sexual activity had better cardiovascular health, fewer depressive symptoms, and enhanced cognitive performance.

Dr. Hui Liu, lead researcher, writes:

"Frequent and enjoyable sex may promote better health by reducing stress, improving sleep, and increasing feelings of well-being." [Liu, H. et al., 2016, Michigan State University]

3. Physical Touch Releases Healing Hormones

During sex, the body releases oxytocin (the "bonding hormone"), dopamine (the "pleasure chemical"), and endorphins (natural painkillers). These chemicals not only foster trust but literally help the body heal, relax, and thrive. Dr. Ian Kerner, a certified sex therapist and author, says:

"Sex can be medicinal. It calms the nervous system, increases intimacy, and helps us feel seen, desired, and safe." [Kerner, I., 2020, *She Comes First*]

Safe Boning

While passion should be unrestrained, it should never be careless — nor unprotected, especially when you are not in a committed relationship that is sexually exclusive. But whether you're married, monogamous or ethically non-monogamous, safe sex is sexy and smart. Safety preserves trust and removes anxiety, allowing your bodies to meet without fear.

Tips for Safe, Soulful Sex

- **Use protection:** Condoms (external and internal), dental dams, or gloves should be used during any penetration or oral-genital contact unless in a mutually monogamous, STI-tested relationship.

- **Get tested regularly:** Even if monogamous, annual screenings ensure peace of mind and mutual respect.

- **Communicate openly:** Talk about boundaries, turn-ons, triggers, and emotional safety before trying new positions or fantasies.

- **Use lube:** Reduce friction, increase pleasure, and prevent micro-tears (especially with adventurous positions).

- **Aftercare matters:** After intense intimacy, hold each other. Hydrate. Check in emotionally. Sex isn't just the act — it's the echo.

Why Lovecation?

This book gives you more than physical positions. It offers:

✓ **62 opportunities to connect in new, vulnerable, erotic ways**

✓ **A 31-day roadmap to rediscover each other's bodies and needs**

✓ **Emotional bridges to reestablish intimacy, joy, and spontaneity**

✓ **A ritual for healing, celebrating, and reigniting your love**

So whether you're lovers rediscovering your fire or soulmates nurturing your spark, let this book guide your next intimate adventure.

Don't just Lovecation for the climax. Do it for the connection with your Chosen, your Love. Lust is empty and is a worthless waste of time, But love! That's the stuff of longevity. After all, that is what we want – the good stuff to last. Not just for the body, but for the bond.

Take the vow. Book your Lovecation with your mate and use this manual as inspiration or as a coach. Either way, you surely will make pleasure a priority again. Have a great fucking time!

Week 1

The Warm-Up
Eye Contact, Connection, Chemistry
(Days 1 - 7)

Welcome to the beginning of your Lovecation. This week is about awakening the senses, reconnecting with the body, and building anticipation with Daily Duets of exciting Love Postures. You're not racing to climax — you're reintroducing yourselves as lovers, playmates, and explorers of each other's desire.

All contrasting Daily Duets feature activities that awaken the senses and engage the mind (as well as other parts of the body). These first pairings lean into eye contact, emotional connection, and sensual closeness.

This first week will get you off with a major bang as it requires you to start this Lovecation being both vulnerable and in full control. Your first challenge will be an exercise in competitive restraint. No climax until both are close, and then the Cum-A-Thon begins to see who can get the most orgasms in during today's session.

Let this week be your invitation to a Lovecation at least once a quarter with your significant other that you hope will stay that way. Give yourself permission this week to be present, involved, connected, seen and felt. Let your skin ask the questions your lips don't dare let fall from them, yet.

Get and give love to each other so fucking good that you both will be singing the Cambell Soup Song anytime you're idle and your mind defaults to your soulmate.

"Mmmmm mmmm good. Mmmm mmmm good."

Sensual Prompt

Before each session, sit close. Hold hands. Look into each other's eyes and ask:

*"What do you crave most
from me today?"*

Don't answer quickly. Let it simmer. Whisper the truth.

Erotic Challenge

Use this week to explore edging, holding back until you're both shaking with need. Learn each other's pleasure peaks. Let the delay increase the depth.

♥

Daily Love Postures:

Let's start this grand time with sexy glances and insatiable stares, words that entice, and actions that are sure to please. Good Loving!

Position #1. Missionary – *A Return to Eye Contact*
There's a reason this classic still reigns. With your bodies aligned and your eyes locked, this is intimacy unfiltered. You kiss, you gaze, you whisper—and the slow thrusts invite soul-level connection.

Position #2. Cowboy – *You Ride, He Watches*
Now reverse the energy. He lies back and you take control—slow at first, then rolling your hips with purpose. It's wild, free, and focused on your pleasure. Let him see what makes you melt.

Position #3. Lotus – *Legs Wrapped, Hearts Tangled*

This upright seated embrace wraps your bodies—and emotions—tightly together. You breathe in tandem. It's tantric, tender, and full of forehead kisses.

Position #4. Doggystyle – *Primal and Powerful*

Hands and knees, you surrender. He grips your hips with hunger. Each thrust is deep, raw, and uninhibited. This isn't about looking—it's about feeling everything.

Position #5. Cowgirl – *The Performer's Throne*
You straddle him—front or reverse—and claim the tempo. He's yours to control. Moans become music. Let your body be the star of the show.

Position #6. Spooning – *Lazy, Loving Entry*
Now rest together, bodies curled, and let him enter from behind with slow, sleepy thrusts. It's warmth, it's safety—it's staying in love's arms long after the climax.

DAY 4

Position #7. T-Position – *Creative Alignment*
Your bodies form a "T," legs at angles, hips locked. This surprising entry provides full friction and room for playful experimentation.

Position #8. Flatiron – *Pressed and Possessed*
You lie flat, stomach down. He presses in, controlling depth and rhythm. The intensity is steady, grounded, and deeply satisfying.

Position #9. Seated Straddle – *Chest to Chest, Lips to Lips*

You sit on his lap, wrap around him, and grind slow. Every kiss lands soft and hot. This is love, lust, and closeness in one long embrace.

Position #10. Face-sitting – *My Throne, Your Worship*

Now you sit above him, dripping confidence. His mouth serves, and your hips guide the rhythm. You're not just in control—you're being adored.

DAY 6

Position #11. Edge of Bed – *Thrust and Grip*
You lie near the bed's edge, and he stands, pulling you in. The angle is intense, the grip is tight, and your moans are involuntary.

Position #12. Kneeling Wrap – *Held and Held Together*
You both kneel upright, legs wrapped around his waist. You rock in harmony. The intimacy is deep, almost meditative.

Position #13. Tabletop – *Bent Over, Owned Fully*
You lean forward onto a firm surface. He enters from behind, gripping your waist. This is animalistic, intense, and fast.

Position #14. Bridge – *Arched for Worship*
You lie back, hips lifted in a graceful arc. He watches, marvels, and enters with reverence. Your body is an altar of pleasure.

Week 1 Quiz:

Week 1 Vibe Check

Describe the energy of these positions in your own words:

_____

_____

_____

_____

_____

_____

_____

_____

💜 Intimacy Score

How connected did you feel during this week as you shared the various Love Postures?

☐ 1 – Distant

☐ 2 – Okay

☐ 3 – Emotionally Aware

☐ 4 – Strong Bond

☐ 5 – Soul-Level Intimacy

😶 Pleasure Score

How pleasurable was Week 1 physically?

☐ 1 – Not Great

☐ 2 – Mild

☐ 3 – Good

☐ 4 – Very Good

☐ 5 – Intense, Mind-Blowing

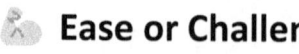 Ease or Challenge

Were this week's Love Postures easy or difficult to execute?

- **Flexibility Needed:** ☐ None ☐ Moderate ☐ Athletic

- **Strength Required:** ☐ Minimal ☐ Some ☐ Full-body effort

- **Balance / Stability:** ☐ Easy ☐ Tricky ☐ Wobbly But Worth It

---

😈 Who took the Lead this week?

☐ I did
☐ My partner did
☐ We traded control
☐ No lead—just flowed

 Best Moment

What was unforgettable about this week's Affection Share?

_____

_____

_____

_____

_____

_____

_____

_____

_____

_____

_____

⟳ Would you do this week's routine again?

☐ Hell yes!

☐ Occasionally

☐ Maybe with a twist

☐ Probably not

Elaborate Your Answer:

_____

_____

_____

_____

_____

_____

_____

_____

💡 Ideas to Enhance It Next Time

(e.g., change location, music, lighting, add a toy, try a different speed, include a mirror...)

💜 Afterglow Words

How did you each feel emotionally and physically after completing this week's Love Fest?

_____

_____

_____

_____

🔥 What concerns need addressing?

_____

_____

_____

_____

_____

_____

💋 FINAL RATING FOR WEEK 1

Draw a heart and fill it in (1 to 5 hearts)

💜 ♡♡♡♡ Not for us

💜 💜 ♡♡♡ Has potential

💜 💜 💜 ♡♡ Worth revisiting

💜 💜 💜 💜 ♡ Favorite material

💜 💜 💜 💜 💜 🔥 Sex Hall of Fame

Week 2

Deepening Desire
Teasing, Power Plays, Creative Control
(Days 8 – 14)

In Week 2, you expand. You tease. You dare. These positions are about flirtation with power—switching control, bending expectations, using space creatively. It's time to blend fantasy with rhythm, to experiment with balance, and to welcome tension that builds toward unforgettable release.

These are the games lovers play when comfort has already been established—and curiosity has taken over. Let's see how many

Love Postures you'll end up adding to these 14 we suggest you definitely enjoy this week.

Sensual Prompt

Begin with a five-minute tease. One person undresses the other... slowly. No sex, no touching genitals. Just watching, touching arms, neck, thighs. Whisper: "I want you, but I'm going to take my time."

Erotic Challenge

Experiment with dominance and submission. Switch roles. One night, you're in control — giving orders, choosing pace. Next night, you surrender completely. Use scarves or hands to guide, restrain, explore. Good Loving!

❤️

Daily Love Postures:

The time has come for variety, erotic teasing, and intimate depth. Push past your norms and get creative, the whole time still staying in just enough control to get nice and comfy so you can relax and get all that Good Loving!

DAY 8

Position #15. Butterfly – *Legs Lifted, Heart Wide*
Your legs rest on his shoulders, hips at the bed's edge. You're open, exposed, and feeling everything. The depth is soul-touching.

Position #16. Lap Dance – *Let Me Tease You*
Now, before any entry—straddle him. Dance. Let your hips grind slow. Let his hands ache to touch. Make him wait. And ache. And beg.

DAY 9

Position #17. Standing – *Urgent, Wall-Pressed Desire*
Against the wall, legs wrapped, arms around his neck—he lifts, you cling. There's no time to undress properly. This is passion that couldn't wait.

Position #18. Suspended – *Lifted Love*
Using strong arms or supportive furniture, he holds you midair. Every thrust is felt doubly—from below, and from the ache in your core.

Position #19. Deep Seated – *Hips &*
Hearts Aligned
Fully clothed or naked, you sit across
from each other, hips touching. Entry is
slow and deep. Movements? Subtle.
Erotic? Completely.

Position #20. Chair Ride – *Ecstasy in*
Every Grind
Now take control. Straddle him in a firm
chair, knees planted, and bounce until he
gasps your name.

DAY 11

Position #21. Side Saddle – *Elegant, Erotic Motion*
You straddle his lap sideways, one arm around his neck. Your thighs squeeze. Your hips roll. It's slow-motion seduction.

Position #22. Crossover – *Twisted in Desire*
One leg over his. Bodies angled. Entry is tight. The friction? Electrifying. The sound? Addictively wet.

Position #23. Scissors – *Locked, Tangled, Groaning*
You lie side-by-side, legs tangled like blades crossing. Each movement is felt along your entire core. It's intimate, tight, and delicious.

Position #24. Face-to-Face Missionary – *Tender, Teasing Gaze*
This isn't about thrusting. It's about whispering. Holding. Watching. Let your bodies move slow—your eyes do the heavy lifting.

Position #25. Prone Bone – *Flattened, Taken Deeply*
You lie flat, back arched slightly. He slides in slowly and holds you down— gently, but completely. This is depth and dominance in harmony.

Position #26. The Arch – *Exhibition of Desire*
You stretch backwards like a dancer in worship. He enters from above, watching you bend and moan with every breath.

Position #27. Cross-Body – *Side Entry, Breasts in Hands*
You lie on your side while he enters from behind, curled against you. His hands slide across your breasts as you move in sync.

Position #28. Dolphin – *Ride the Curve*
You arch your back and brace your hands. He rides the wave of your body, curved like ocean motion. This one is wild—let it take you.

Week 2 Quiz:

🔥 Week 2 Vibe Check

Describe the energy of these positions in your own words:

_____

_____

_____

_____

_____

_____

_____

_____

_____

💜 Intimacy Score

How connected did you feel during this week as you shared the various Love Postures?

☐ 1 – Distant

☐ 2 – Okay

☐ 3 – Emotionally Aware

☐ 4 – Strong Bond

☐ 5 – Soul-Level Intimacy

😲 Pleasure Score

How pleasurable was Week 2 physically?

☐ 1 – Not Great

☐ 2 – Mild

☐ 3 – Good

☐ 4 – Very Good

☐ 5 – Intense, Mind-Blowing

 Ease or Challenge

Were this week's Love Postures easy or difficult to execute?

- **Flexibility Needed:** ☐ None ☐ Moderate ☐ Athletic

- **Strength Required:** ☐ Minimal ☐ Some ☐ Full-body effort

- **Balance / Stability:** ☐ Easy ☐ Tricky ☐ Wobbly But Worth It

---

🦉 Who took the Lead this week?

☐ I did

☐ My partner did

☐ We traded control

☐ No lead—just flowed

✦ Best Moment

What was unforgettable about this week's Affection Share?

_____

_____

_____

_____

_____

_____

_____

_____

_____

_____

_____

🔄 Would you do this week's routine again?

☐ Hell yes!

☐ Occasionally

☐ Maybe with a twist

☐ Probably not

Elaborate Your Answer:

_____

_____

_____

_____

_____

_____

_____

_____

💡 Ideas to Enhance It Next Time

(e.g., change location, music, lighting, add a toy, try a different speed, include a mirror…)

💜 Afterglow Words

How did you each feel emotionally and physically after completing this week's Love Fest?

_____

_____

_____

_____

🔥 What concerns need addressing?

_____

_____

_____

_____

_____

💋 FINAL RATING FOR WEEK 2

Draw a heart and fill it in (1 to 5 hearts)

💜 ♡♡♡♡ Not for us

💜 💜 ♡♡♡ Has potential

💜 💜 💜 ♡♡ Worth revisiting

💜 💜 💜 💜 ♡ Favorite material

💜 💜 💜 💜 💜 🔥 Sex Hall of Fame

Week 3

The Body Electric
Rhythm, Motion, Sensory Indulgence
(Days 15 – 21)

Now, let's switch it up and start mixing it up. This is the third week of "Duets" but this and all remaining weeks will still offer pleasant surprises sure to please and help you break free of the same-ole-same-old routine. I'm sure, by now, you've probably already started your own set of 2-a-days and I'm the one late to the party!

For those arriving with me, these final weeks of pairing a dominant position and a submissive position each day will not be a waste. These pairings were carefully considered to position you for optimal stimulation. Each day's Love Postures will deliver the playful and the serious (an intimate and an adventurous) position.

This week is about movement and all of it is a show of possibility for your pleasure — rocking, riding, lifting, bouncing. Give yourself permission to take chances and move outside your usual ways. If you don't normally dance with your mate, make this the week you dance together for the first time. Let your bodies dance with desire. Good Loving!

Sensual Prompt

Before you partake, explore each other's bodies with only your fingertips and lips for ten minutes. No penetration. No words. Just sound, breath, sensation.

Erotic Challenge

Add one easy sensory element to your foreplay this week Try somethings like this again because you probably haven't pulled out these classic moves since you first started loving on each other:

- Ice cubes dragged along thighs

- Warm oil dripped on the lower back

- Blindfolds to heighten anticipation

- Music with deep bass to sync movement

♥

Daily Love Postures:

Now, it's time for melodic cadences, uninhibited motion, and sensual play. Good Loving!

Position #29. Edge of Bed – *Pelvic Power*
You lie at the edge, hips hanging just enough. He grips your thighs and pulls you into him—deep and rhythmic.

▼ *Submissive energy: open, stretched, accessible.*

Position #30. Butterfly – *Heart-Wide, Legs-High*
Your legs rise and rest on his shoulders, your hips supported by the bed's edge or a pillow. Each thrust lifts you closer to euphoria.

▲ *Powerful gaze. Exposed. Sacred.*

Position #31. Lap Dance – *Tease Until Taken*
Fully clothed or barely dressed, you straddle him, roll your hips, and make him beg. He can't enter—yet. The anticipation is the aphrodisiac.

▼ *Playful dominance. Command the tempo.*

Position #32. Suspended – *Adventurous Support*
Held midair or braced against a strong surface—legs wrapped around, arms gripping—you feel weightless. Every thrust is gravity-defying pleasure.

▲ *Trust. Strength. Need.*

Position #33. Chair Ride – *Seated Ecstasy*
You face each other in a sturdy chair. His hands slide under your thighs, and you ride like you're dancing to a silent rhythm only your bodies hear.

▼ *Connection-rich. Slow or wild—it's your choice.*

Position #34. Deep Seated – *Perfect Alignment*
Hips flush. Breathing synced. You grind in circles, bodies melted into one. This is slow-burning fire, perfect for mutual orgasms.

▲ *Sacred geometry of love.*

Position #35. Crossover – *Twisted and Tight*
A side entry with a twist—your leg over his, bodies angled for perfect friction. It's intimate and surprising.

▼ *Unique angles. Tight squeezes.*

Position #36. The Arch – *Your Body, My Altar*
You bend backwards, offering your chest, neck, and core. He watches you arch and receives you with reverence and hunger.

▲ *Visual beauty. Worshipful energy.*

Position #37. Standing Split – *One Leg Up, Heat Rising*
You lift one leg high—over his shoulder or up on furniture—while he grips and enters. This is primal control.

▼ *Flexibility meets dominance.*

Position #38. Face-to-Face Missionary – *Eye-Locked Devotion*
Soft kisses, whispers, full presence. No distractions—just you and him, as if nothing else matters.

▲ *Soul penetration.*

Position #39. Prone Bone – *Laid Down and Taken Deep*
You lie flat on your belly, hips slightly lifted. He enters deep, slow, powerful. This is one of the deepest strokes you'll feel.

▼ *Quiet surrender.*

Position #40. X Marks the Spot – *Crossed Legs, Craved Entry*
You lock your legs in a crisscross. The friction builds and targets intense zones. It's different—and it's divine.

▲ *New territory.*

DAY 21

Position #41. Side Saddle – *Erotic Elegance*

You straddle him sideways, your legs over his lap. One hand on his shoulder, the other exploring your own curves.

▼ *Graceful and slow.*

Position #42. Scissors – *Tight and Tangled*

Both lying side-by-side, legs interlaced like blades in motion. Friction is full. Closeness is unavoidable.

▲ *Entanglement of heat.*

Week 3 Quiz:

🔥 **Week 3 Vibe Check**

Describe the energy of these positions in your own words:

_____

_____

_____

_____

_____

_____

_____

_____

_____

💕 Intimacy Score

How connected did you feel during this week as you shared the various Love Postures?

- ☐ 1 – Distant
- ☐ 2 – Okay
- ☐ 3 – Emotionally Aware
- ☐ 4 – Strong Bond
- ☐ 5 – Soul-Level Intimacy

😲 Pleasure Score

How pleasurable was Week 3 physically?

- ☐ 1 – Not Great
- ☐ 2 – Mild
- ☐ 3 – Good
- ☐ 4 – Very Good
- ☐ 5 – Intense, Mind-Blowing

Ease or Challenge

Were this week's Love Postures easy or difficult to execute?

- **Flexibility Needed:** ☐ None ☐ Moderate ☐ Athletic

- **Strength Required:** ☐ Minimal ☐ Some ☐ Full-body effort

- **Balance / Stability:** ☐ Easy ☐ Tricky ☐ Wobbly But Worth It

---

😼 Who took the Lead this week?

☐ I did
☐ My partner did
☐ We traded control
☐ No lead—just flowed

 **Best Moment**

What was unforgettable about this week's Affection Share?

🔄 Would you do this week's routine again?

☐ Hell yes!

☐ Occasionally

☐ Maybe with a twist

☐ Probably not

Elaborate Your Answer:

_____

_____

_____

_____

_____

_____

_____

_____

💡 Ideas to Enhance It Next Time

(e.g., change location, music, lighting, add a toy, try a different speed, include a mirror...)

💜 Afterglow Words

How did you each feel emotionally and physically after completing this week's Love Fest?

_____

_____

_____

_____

🔥 What concerns need addressing?

_____

_____

_____

_____

_____

_____

💋 FINAL RATING FOR WEEK 3

Draw a heart and fill it in (1 to 5 hearts)

💜 ♡♡♡♡ Not for us

💜 💜 ♡♡♡ Has potential

💜 💜 💜 ♡♡ Worth revisiting

💜 💜 💜 💜 ♡ Favorite material

💜 💜 💜 💜 💜 🔥 Sex Hall of Fame

Week 4

The Erotic Unknown
New Angles, Full Surrender,
Bold Adventure
(Days 22 – 28)

This week, we want to remember to stay hydrated better than in the past weeks because we will not be slacking off on our Daily Duets. We joke that we definitely don't want to have people thinking we're vampires because we're not being seen much during the day due to being caught up in the rapture of love (like Anita Baker says, "nothing else can compare"), so we have to at least go out during the morning one day this week and then during the afternoon another day this week just to see what this city is offering before our honeymoon is over.

All in all, I'm sure your experiences have been mind-blowing! You've likely pulled out your Karma Sutra and explored even further. Nice! Great initiative! Be sure to do whatever you two agree to and enjoy adding during this week's Love Postures too.

Sensual Prompt:

"What have you fantasized about . . . but never told me?"

Ask this question of each other, After one asks this question and it is answered, the other asks this question and receives an answer. Now, you two are on the same page and can spend the week bringing those secret cravings into light. Even a small gesture can fulfill a large desire.

Erotic Challenge:

Try one new environment. The shower. The floor. A chair. The backyard under moonlight. Change the space, and the energy changes with it. Take your Lovecation off the bed.

♥

Daily Love Postures:

Now, it's time for bold discovery, bold positions, and breaking routines. Good Loving!

DAY 22

Position #43. Dolphin – *Upward Curve, Wild Ride*
You lie arched, hips lifted like a wave. His body presses from above, each thrust curling your toes.
▼ *Curved and intense.*

Position #44. Cross-Body – *Side Entry, Sensual Breast Play*
He enters from the side as your body folds toward him. His hand cups your breast. The motion is smooth, sensual.
▲ *Breast-forward bliss.*

Position #45. The Rocker – *Slow Grind, Divine Rhythm*
You sit facing, rocking together like waves in sync. No hard thrusts—just deep, controlled pleasure.

▼ *Shared tempo.*

Position #46. Cowgirl Lean Back – *Back Arched, Orgasmic Stretch*
You lean back on his thighs, riding slow and low. The stretch deepens penetration and eye contact.

▲ *Seductive control.*

Position #47. Modified Doggy – *Pillow Under Hips, More Depth*
With your hips raised just right, he enters with new intensity. The angle is sharper, the groans deeper.

▼ *Amplified submission.*

Position #48. Side-by-Side – *Slow, Silky, Breath-Sharing*
You lie facing each other, moving as one. Hips grind lazily. Tongues explore slowly.

▲ *Soft-core heaven.*

Position #49. The Scoop – *Curled in Close*

He holds you from behind, bodies curved like commas. His pelvis moves with subtle power.

▼ *Soft dominance.*

Position #50. Standing Wrap – *Kiss Me and Take Me*

Legs locked around his waist, back against the wall, hands in hair. This is desperate romance.

▲ *Urgent heat.*

Position #51. Shower Love – *Slippery and Wet*

Water cascades down while your bodies glide into each other. You lean into the tile. His hands explore with purpose.

▼ *Wet surrender.*

Position #52. Lazy Dog – *Laid Back Doggy, Slow and Deep*

No rush. No thrusts. Just deep entry and prolonged eye-closing pleasure.

▲ *Dreamy and decadent.*

DAY 27

Position #53. Mattress Monarch – *Treat Me Like Royalty*
You lie back, limbs relaxed. He adores every inch of you. Oral, kisses, entry... you're worshipped like a goddess.

▼ *Sensual throne.*

Position #54. The Slide – *Wet and Slippery Full-Body Glide*
Bodies oiled and pressed together—thigh to thigh, skin to skin—you slide over each other like silk.

▲ *Erotic messiness.*

DAY 28

Position #55. G-Whiz – *Legs Up, Tilted for G-Spot Glory*
Legs high and wide, hips tilted. He hits the right spot again and again. Your moans echo off the walls.

▼ *Intentional bliss.*

Position #Position #56. The Tangle –
Limbs Everywhere, Passion Unleashed
No position, just passion. You wrap and twist in chaotic harmony. This is a collision of love and lust.

▲ *Beautiful chaos.*

Week 4 Quiz:

◌ Week 4 Vibe Check

Describe the energy of these positions in your own words:

_____

_____

_____

_____

_____

_____

_____

_____

_____

💜 Intimacy Score

How connected did you feel during this week as you shared the various Love Postures?

☐ 1 – Distant

☐ 2 – Okay

☐ 3 – Emotionally Aware

☐ 4 – Strong Bond

☐ 5 – Soul-Level Intimacy

😶 Pleasure Score

How pleasurable was Week 4 physically?

☐ 1 – Not Great

☐ 2 – Mild

☐ 3 – Good

☐ 4 – Very Good

☐ 5 – Intense, Mind-Blowing

 Ease or Challenge

Were this week's Love Postures easy or difficult to execute?

- **Flexibility Needed:** ☐ None ☐ Moderate ☐ Athletic

- **Strength Required:** ☐ Minimal ☐ Some ☐ Full-body effort

- **Balance / Stability:** ☐ Easy ☐ Tricky ☐ Wobbly But Worth It

---

🐱 Who took the Lead this week?

☐ I did
☐ My partner did
☐ We traded control
☐ No lead—just flowed

 **Best Moment**

What was unforgettable about this week's Affection Share?

_____

_____

_____

_____

_____

_____

_____

_____

_____

_____

🔄 Would you do this week's routine again?

☐ Hell yes!

☐ Occasionally

☐ Maybe with a twist

☐ Probably not

Elaborate Your Answer:

_____

_____

_____

_____

_____

_____

_____

_____

 **Ideas to Enhance It Next Time**

(e.g., change location, music, lighting, add a toy, try a different speed, include a mirror...)

_____

_____

_____

_____

_____

_____

_____

_____

_____

_____

_____

💜 Afterglow Words

How did you each feel emotionally and physically after completing this week's Love Fest?

_____

_____

_____

_____

🔥 What concerns need addressing?

_____

_____

_____

_____

_____

_____

💋 FINAL RATING FOR WEEK 4

Draw a heart and fill it in (1 to 5 hearts)

🖤 ♡♡♡♡ Not for us

🖤 🖤 ♡♡♡ Has potential

🖤 🖤 🖤 ♡♡ Worth revisiting

🖤 🖤 🖤 🖤 ♡ Favorite material

🖤 🖤 🖤 🖤 🖤 💧 Sex Hall of Fame

Week 5

The Fanned Flames
Slow Burn, Adoration, Sacred Sensuality
(Days 29-31)

Now, let's switch it up and start mixing it up. This is the first week of "Duets" and all remaining weeks will follow the same routine. I'm sure, by now, you've probably already started your own set of 2-a-days and I'm the one late to the party!

Sensual Prompt

Tonight, don't have sex . . . make love. Start with a slow bath or shower. Wash each other's hair. Dry each other with warm towels. Then, lay naked, skin-to-skin, and breathe together for 2 minutes before beginning.

Erotic Challenge

A 3-hour lovemaking session. Set the mood: music, low lights, wine or tea. Explore foreplay, two positions, a nap or rest, then wake for more. Touch between the touches. Kiss between the words. End with the final position: The Stillness. Just hold. Just feel. Just be.

♥

Daily Love Postures:

Now, it's time for the deepest love, tantric joy, and explosive surrender. Good Loving!

DAY 29

Position #57. Melt – *Full-Body Sweat, Deep Penetration*
Pressed chest to chest, skin-on-skin, hips in perfect sync. You melt into each other—wet, wild, holy.

▼ *Total union.*

Position #58. The Kissed Back – *Pleasure Poured Down Your Spine*
Lying face down, he licks, kisses, bites. Each touch builds until he enters from behind, gentle and ravenous.

▲ *Sweet torment.*

DAY 30

Position #59. The Tease – *Fast-Then-Slow, Just-Enough Entry*
He slides in barely... then pulls back. You beg. He smiles. This is sensual control, and you're loving every second.

▼ *Anticipation domination.*

Position #60. Table Face-Down – *Furniture Fantasy Fulfilled*
Bent over the table, hands gripping edge. No words, just movement, impact, surrender.

▲ *Raw elegance.*

Position #61. The Press – *Full Body Weight, One Last Ride*
He lowers into you slowly, his chest pinning you with warmth. The rhythm is slow, inevitable.

▼ *Still waters run deep.*

Position #62. The Stillness – *No Motion. No Words. Just Being.*
He's inside. You don't move. You just breathe. Feel him throb. Feel yourself open. The ultimate surrender.

▲ *Transcendence.*

Week 5 Quiz:

🔥 Week 5 Vibe Check

Describe the energy of these positions in your own words:

_____

_____

_____

_____

_____

_____

_____

_____

_____

💕 Intimacy Score

How connected did you feel during this week
as you shared the various Love Postures?

☐ 1 – Distant

☐ 2 – Okay

☐ 3 – Emotionally Aware

☐ 4 – Strong Bond

☐ 5 – Soul-Level Intimacy

😻 Pleasure Score

How pleasurable was Week 5 physically?

☐ 1 – Not Great

☐ 2 – Mild

☐ 3 – Good

☐ 4 – Very Good

☐ 5 – Intense, Mind-Blowing

 Ease or Challenge

Were this week's Love Postures easy or difficult to execute?

- **Flexibility Needed:** ☐ None ☐ Moderate ☐ Athletic

- **Strength Required:** ☐ Minimal ☐ Some ☐ Full-body effort

- **Balance / Stability:** ☐ Easy ☐ Tricky ☐ Wobbly But Worth It

---

😺 Who took the Lead this week?

☐ I did
☐ My partner did
☐ We traded control
☐ No lead—just flowed

 **Best Moment**

What was unforgettable about this week's Affection Share?

🔁 Would you do this week's routine again?

☐ Hell yes!

☐ Occasionally

☐ Maybe with a twist

☐ Probably not

Elaborate Your Answer:

_____

_____

_____

_____

_____

_____

_____

_____

💡 Ideas to Enhance It Next Time

(e.g., change location, music, lighting, add a toy, try a different speed, include a mirror...)

💜 Afterglow Words

How did you each feel emotionally and physically after completing this week's Love Fest?

_____

_____

_____

_____

💧 What concerns need addressing?

_____

_____

_____

_____

_____

_____

💋 FINAL RATING FOR WEEK 5

Draw a heart and fill it in (1 to 5 hearts)

💜 ♡♡♡♡ Not for us

💜 💜 ♡♡♡ Has potential

💜 💜 💜 ♡♡ Worth revisiting

💜 💜 💜 💜 ♡ Favorite material

💜 💜 💜 💜 💜 🌢 Sex Hall of Fame

Arrived

Let The Fireworks Commence
New View, Stronger Bond, Best Mate

These 31 days are more than just a challenge. They're a foundation for a lifetime of erotic connection — an erotic holiday gift perfectly packaged in an easy-to-reference style that will find use for you and your mate more than once. You no longer have to feel pressure or restriction when it's time to be your most vulnerable.

You now have 62 ways to say, "I want you."

The Lovecation Lifestyle
Make Love Your Destination

What if passion didn't have to fade?

What if you could return to that place where time slows, hearts beat faster, and you look at each other like it's the first—and last— time, every time?

That place exists. It's not a hotel. Not a weekend trip. It's a Lovecation — an erotic escape that begins the moment you choose each other... with full attention, full presence, and full-body love.

A New Way to Love: 31 Days of Intimacy

These 31 days were not just a challenge. They were a reawakening.

You didn't just explore 62 positions. You Lovers actually:

- Took control and surrendered.

- Teased and worshipped.

- Discovered new angles of joy—and rediscovered each other's depths.

- Got messy, got slow, got loud, got still.

You made your bed a sacred site. You made time your servant, not your thief. You made your lover feel chosen again and again. This is the Lovecation Lifestyle.

Imagine if every month, you booked exclusive time like this with your Lover. Imagine how much better your relationship will be if you valued it enough to regularly book time off from work during the year to be sure your mate knows their love is appreciated, desired and required. Imagine if you planned:

- Nights of no phones, no emails—only skin-on-skin conversations.

- Days where sex wasn't a quick release but a journey through power, softness, and sweat.

- Moments where you remembered why you chose each other in the first place... and chose again.

You don't need a passport. You just need a promise: "I will meet you here. Body, heart, and soul."

62 Positions: Your Erotic Compass

Use these 62 positions not as a checklist—but as a playlist. Let each pairing guide your mood:

- Feeling wild? Try **Standing Split** and **The Slide**.

- Craving closeness? Go for **Spooning** and **The Stillness**.

- Need to laugh while climaxing? Nothing beats **The Saddle** and **Lap Dance**.

- Want to cry from connection? Let **Lotus** and **Melt** carry you.

Mix them. Revisit them. Invent new ones. Let your bedroom become a playground, a temple, a secret garden.. Make your erotic ritual a sacred moment of refuge exclusively reserved for you Lovers. Here's how to turn sex into soul fuel:

1. **Set the Space.** Low lights, warm sheets, music that moves you. A clean room can change everything.

2. **Set the Intention.** Choose your two positions. Speak them aloud. Make a vow: "Tonight, I give you my full presence."

3. **Set Each Other Free.** Let there be no shame, no rush, no performance. Only pleasure, patience, and praise.

Go Deeper

Here are 4 ways to keep the Lovecation going:

1. **Start a Passion Journal.** After each night, write 3 things you loved. Ask each other: What do I want more of?

2. **Use the Erotic Dice.** One die for positions. One die for locations. One die for speed or style. Roll and surrender.

3. **Take a Real Lovecation.** Book a hotel. Pack lingerie. Do 4 positions a day. Sleep, laugh, eat, make love again.

4. **Create Fantasy Nights.** Roleplay. Dress up. Speak new names. Fulfill one unspoken desire every week.

Your Lovecation Invitation

Taking up the challenge offered by this literary offering is the only way to book your Lovecation and actually make the trip. Do it now! You deserve this. Your relationship deserves it. Your body deserves to be explored, appreciated, devoured, embraced — not just when it's convenient, but when it's intentional. So don't just read this book. Live it.

⊞ Pick your month.

◉ Choose your location, or make your bedroom your playground.

📖 Open this book to Page 1.

💋 Begin again.

The time for love is now. The place is here. And the Lover . . . your mate . . . is still the one you choose every time. Say it out loud: "I only want you." Now show it, every single day.

Experience your Lovecation today! Remember, this is more than a manual —it's a challenge. It's a celebration. And, it is indeed a sensual lifestyle.

Plan your escape: 31 days, 62 positions, unlimited pleasure, infinite memories made. Imagine a seaside villa, a mountain lodge, or your cozy bedroom. Declare this month for your love. Use your time for rediscovery. Indulge in your lust for your spouse. Bask in that Good Loving! Keep thanking God for loving affection. For tenderness. And for sweat, moans, laughter, and orgasmic release with your soulmate because you didn't need a passport to travel into each other. Come again real soon! Enjoy your LOVECATION!

References

Foreword Footnotes, Format, Resources

Herewith is a "Reference List" and formatted "Footnotes" section to reinforce the *Foreword* of *LOVECATION: 31 Days, 62 Positions.* This will provide credibility, professionalism, and structure those engaging in conversations with others about the initiatives presented in this project may find especially valuable.

FOOTNOTES

1. Lehmiller, J. (2021). "What Happens When Couples Stop Having Sex?" *Kinsey Confidential*, Kinsey Institute.

2. Liu, H., Waite, L., Shen, S., & Wang, D. (2016). "Is Sex Good for Your Health? A National Study on Partnered Sexuality and Cardiovascular Risk among Older Men and Women." *Journal of Health and Social Behavior*, 57(3), 276–296.

3. Kerner, I. (2020). *She Comes First: The Thinking Man's Guide to Pleasuring a Woman*. Harper Wave.

REFERENCE LIST

(APA-style citations for professional formatting)

Lehmiller, J. J. (2021). *What Happens When Couples Stop Having Sex?* Kinsey Institute. Retrieved from https://www.kinseyinstitute.org/research/publications.php

Liu, H., Waite, L. J., Shen, S., & Wang, D. H. (2016). Is sex good for your health? A national study on partnered sexuality and cardiovascular risk among older men and women. *Journal of Health and Social Behavior*, 57(3), 276–296. https://doi.org/10.1177/0022146516661597

Kerner, I. (2020). *She Comes First: The Thinking Man's Guide to Pleasuring a Woman* (Revised Edition). New York, NY: Harper Wave.

www.ingramcontent.com/pod-product-compliance
Lightning Source LLC
Chambersburg PA
CBHW051145020726
47501CB00005B/1684